Phoebe's Sweater

By Joanna Johnson
Illustrated by Eric Johnson

SLATE
FALLS
PRESS

Slate Falls Press, LLC
P.O. Box 7062
Loveland, CO 80537
www.slatefallspress.com

Library of Congress Cataloging-in-Publication Data Johnson, Joanna.
Phoebe's Sweater / by Joanna Johnson illustrations by Eric Johnson
ISBN 978-0-578-04697-6 ISBN 578-04697-0
Library of Congress Control Number: 2010900057
Signature Book Printing, inc.
www.sbpbooks.com

for Laurel

One fall day, when the air was crisp and the wind was cool and the leaves were crunchy under her feet, Phoebe went out to play.

On this particular day, the mailman brought a package for her mother which was a box full of beautiful yarn. Her mother was planning to knit a new sweater for Phoebe to wear next year.

Phoebe's mother spent lots of time reading and studying the perfect pattern for the sweater. Phoebe spent lots of time playing outside while the weather was still nice.

It began to grow cold outside and everyone was busy preparing for winter. Phoebe's mom told her some important news. There would be a new baby in their home this coming summer. Phoebe sat and thought and wondered what babies were like.

Phoebe's mom needed to rest a little more than usual. She kept herself busy working on the new sweater. Phoebe's dad had lots of good ideas for fun wintertime things to do.

Time passed, and soon the snows of winter would begin to lighten. Phoebe started looking forward to spring, warm weather, and being able to play outside in her bare feet again.

Finally, the snow melted completely, and Phoebe was able to go out and play by herself. It was so nice to be outside without her heavy coat, she did not mind the rain one bit.

One summer day, when Phoebe had been playing in the sprinkler, her mother came to her. Her sweater was all finished! She tried it on and it was just right.

The days of summer stretched long and longer, and Phoebe went to stay with her grandparents while her mom and dad waited for the new baby to arrive.

Many exciting things happened that summer...

... and Phoebe forgot all about her new sweater...

...until one fall day, when the air was crisp and the wind was cool and the leaves were crunchy under her feet, Phoebe went out to play.

the end

knitting patterns

Phoebe's Sweater

Size 2 [4, 6] (shown in size 2 and size 6)

Finished Measurements Chest: 25 [27, 29] inches

Yarn

Brown Sheep Company Lamb's Pride Superwash Bulky [100% wool; 110yd/101m per 100g skein]; 6 [8, 9] skeins. Shown in Cinnamon Twist for size 2, in Mint Cream for size 6.

Needles

1 set US 10 ½ double-pointed needles or size to obtain correct gauge

24 inch US 10 ½ circular needle or size to obtain correct gauge

Notions

Stitch holders, removable stitch markers

3- 1 1/4" buttons

Gauge

14 sts/16 rows = 4 inches in stockinette stitch

Pattern Notes

This is a seamless sweater knit starting at the hemline. The simple slip-stitch pattern does most of the shaping for the garment. The best way to select the right size for this sweater is to use the child's chest measurement and add 2-3 inches for positive ease. It is very simple to modify the length of the body and sleeves of this sweater by lengthening or shortening in the plain stockinette sections found above the hem and above the sleeve trim. For example, I knitted the size 6 sweater for my daughter who is 8 years old. I simply added an inch to the sleeve length and to the hood length to customize the fit. Feel free to add an inch or two to the sleeve length- you may gain an extra year of wear out of the sweater this way, as it is the wrist which seems to show first on rapidly growing children in long sleeves, and the pattern looks just fine turned up at the cuff.

Pattern

Body

Using circular needle, cast on 128[140,152] stitches.

Begin 4 row "stripes and bands" slip-stitch pattern:

Row 1: p2, *wyib, sl 1 as if to knit, bring yarn to front and p2*; repeat from * to *

Row 2: k2, *wyif, sl 1 as if to purl, bring yarn to back and k2*; repeat from * to *

Row 3: knit

Row 4: purl

Repeat these 4 rows 5[6,7] times more.

Switch to st st and work straight for 8[10,12] inches more (or desired length), ending with a knit row.

Shape bodice: p 1[2, 4]; *p2tog, p1*; repeat from * to* to last 1[3,4] stitches; p 1[3, 4]. 86[95,104]st remaining.

Work rows 1-4 of pattern, then work rows 1 and 2 of pattern.

First buttonhole row: k3, BO2, knit to end.

Next buttonhole row: p to BO st, CO2, p3.

Work rows 1-4 of pattern 2[3,4] times more, then work rows 1 and 2 of pattern.

Repeat the two buttonhole rows as above.

Work row 1 of pattern.

Divide for sleeves: continuing in patt, work 22[24,26] place on holder; work 42[47,52] place on holder; work 22[24,26].

Front

Make right front, working back and forth on remaining 22[24,26] stitches.

Knit 1 row.

Purl 1 row.

Keeping in pattern as established, work rows 1-4 of pattern 1[2,3] times.

Work rows 1 and 2 of pattern.

Repeat the two buttonhole rows as above.

Work rows 1-4 of pattern.

Keeping in pattern, BO 3, work to end. Work one row. BO3 at beginning of next row, place removable marker or safety pin (this is to mark for the hood placement later on), work to end. Work one row. BO3 at beginning of row. 13[15,17] st remaining. Work 4 rows in pattern, place on holder for shoulder seam.

Make left front by working the 22[24,26] st from the other side. Work in pattern the same as the right side, omitting buttonholes and reversing shaping: 13[15,17] on holder for shoulder seam.

Back

Working on remaining 42[47,52] st from last holder, work in pattern until 1 row shorter than front. Work 13[15,17], place on dpn for shoulder seam; BO16[17,18]; work 13[15,17], place on dpn for shoulder seam.

Finish shoulder seams on each side using 3-needle bind-off.

Sleeves

Make sleeves using dpns by picking up and knitting 30[36,42] st around armhole opening. Mark beg of round. Work st st (knit every round) in round on dpns for 5[6,7] inches.

Decrease round: *k8[10,5], k2tog* repeat from * to* to end of round. 27[33,36] st.

Switch to stripes and bands pattern in the round as follows:

Round 1: *wyib, sl 1 as if to k, bring yarn to front and p2*; repeat from * to* to end of round.

Round 2: *wyib, sl 1 as if to p, bring yarn to front and p2*; repeat from * to* to end of round.

Rounds 3 & 4: knit.

Work in pattern for 5[6,6] inches or to desired length, ending on round 2 of pattern. BO in pattern. Repeat for other sleeve.

Hood

Between the removable markers at the neck edge neatly pick up 44[48,52] stitches. I like to use a crochet hook for this task. With the rs facing you, begin the hood at the right front edge.

Set-up Row: sl1 wyib as if to k, p2, sl1 wyib as if to k, p2, sl1 wyib as if to k, k12[14,16] st, pm, k6, pm, k12[14,16] sl1 wyib as if to k, p2, sl1 wyib as if to k, p2, sl1wyib as if to k.

Next Row: sl1 wyif as if to p, k2, sl1 wyif as if to p, k2, sl1 wyif as if to p, p to last 7 st and sl1 wyif as if to p, k2, sl1 wyif as if to p, k2, sl1 wyif as if to p.

Row 1: knit to first marker, m1, slip marker, knit to next marker, slip marker, m1, knit to the end.

Row 2: purl.

Row 3: sl1 wyib as if to k, p2, sl1 wyib as if to k, p2, sl1 wyib as if to k, knit to first marker, m1, slip marker, knit to next marker, slip marker, m1, knit to last 7 stitches, sl1 wyib as if to k, p2, sl1 wyib as if to k, p2, sl1 wyib as if to k.

Row 4: sl1 wyif as if to purl, k2, sl1 wyif as if to p, k2, sl1 wyif as if to p, purl to last 7 st and sl1 wyif as if to p, k2, sl1 wyif as if to p, k2, sl 1 wyif as if to p.

Repeat these four rows 3[4,4] times more. 60[68,72] st remaining.

Keeping the pattern on the hood edge as worked in these 4 rows, work straight without shaping for another 6.5[6.5,7] inches or to desired length.

Place half of hood st on another needle and graft top of hood using kitchener st.

Finishing

Weave in ends. Block. Sew on buttons.

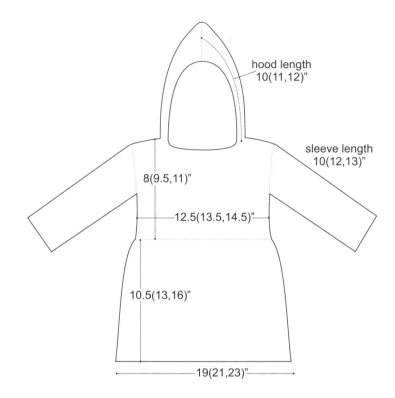

hood length
10(11,12)"

sleeve length
10(12,13)"

8(9.5,11)"

12.5(13.5,14.5)"

10.5(13,16)"

19(21,23)"

Phoebe Mouse

Finished Size 16" tall

Yarn

MC- Brown Sheep Company Lamb's Pride Superwash Worsted, 200y/100g, color: Oats 'N Cream, 1 skein

CC-Brown Sheep Company Lamb's Pride Superwash Worsted, 200y/100g, color: Strawberry Chiffon, 1 skein

Needles

1 set US 5 double-pointed needles or size to obtain correct

   gauge

11 inch US 7 circular needles (or set of US 7 dpns and 16 inch

   circular needles)

Gauge

5 stitches per inch in st st on size US 5 needles

Notions

Stitch markers

Toy stuffing of your choice- polyfill, roving, or a blend is fine

Scraps of wool felt and embroidery thread for doll face

Pattern Notes

Phoebe Mouse is a nearly seamless knit worked in the round, except for her ears, which are worked back and forth and stitched on at the end. This doll pattern is written to be worked on four double-pointed needles; the stitches are divided among three needles leaving the fourth as the working needle.

Feel free to embellish her face as pictured here, or, in a style all your own. My test knitters were very creative and added whiskers, hair bows, button eyes (be sure to sew them very securely for safety reasons), and sweet little mouths.

Pattern

Make head: With size 5 dpns and MC, CO 6 stitches. Divide evenly on three needles. Pm and join for working in the round.

Knit 1 rnd.

Next rnd: *M1, k1* repeat. 12 st.

Next rnd: *M1, k2* repeat. 18 st. Knit 1 rnd.

Next rnd: *M1, k3* repeat. 24 st. Knit 1 rnd.

Next rnd: *M1, k4* repeat. 30 st. Knit 1 rnd.

Next rnd: *M1, k5* repeat. 36 st. Knit 1 rnd.

Next rnd: *M1, k6* repeat. 42 st. Knit 1 rnd.

Next rnd: *M1, k7* repeat. 48 st.

Knit 10 rounds.

Next rnd: *ssk, k6, k2tog, k6* repeat. 42 st rem.

Knit 1 rnd.

Next rnd: *ssk, k5, k2tog, k5* repeat. 36. st rem.

Knit 1 rnd.

Next rnd: *ssk, k4, k2tog, k4* repeat. 30 st rem.

Knit 1 rnd.

Next rnd: *ssk, k3, k2tog, k3* repeat. 24 st rem.

Next rnd: *ssk, k2, k2tog, k2* repeat. 18 st rem.

Next rnd: *ssk, k1, k2tog, k1* repeat. 12 st rem.

Make body:

First rnd: *kfb, k1* repeat. 18 st.

Next rnd: *kfb, k2* repeat. 24 st.

Next rnd: *kfb, k3* repeat. 30 st.

Next rnd: *kfb, k4* repeat. 36 st.

Next rnd: *kfb, k5* repeat. 42 st.

Next rnd: *kfb, k6* repeat. 48 st.

Knit 4 rounds.

Make arm openings:

k 16 (needle 1); k 8 and sl to a holder, k8 (needle 2); k8, k8 and sl to a holder (needle 3).

Next rnd: k16 (needle 1). CO 8 and slip to empty needle, use this needle to k8 from needle 2 (needle 2). K8, CO 8 (needle 3). 48 st.

Knit 26 rounds, leaving arm opening stitches on holders to be picked up later on.

Shape bottom and make leg openings:

K8, m1, k1, m1, knit rest of rnd. 50 st.

Next rnd: k7 and sl to a holder, k4, k7 and sl to a holder; *k2tog* 7 times, k4, *k2tog* 7 times. 22 st.

Next rnd: CO 7 and slip to empty needle, k4, CO 7 (needle 1). k9 (needle 2). k9 (needle 3). 36 st.

Knit 2 rnds even. 36 st.

Slip 9 st from needle 3 to needle 2. Place needle 1 next to needle 2 and graft st using the kitchener st. Weave in ends, lightly block head and body, then stuff the head and body.

Make arms:

Slip 8 st from holder onto dp needle. Pick up 12 st around arm opening. Join and knit every rnd for 34 rnds. Cut yarn, leaving a 10 inch tail, loosely thread through stitches, lightly block arm. Stuff arm, stuffing joint loosely for flexibility, and cinch opening, weaving in ends when finished.

Repeat for the other arm.

Make legs:

Slip 7 stitches from holder onto dp needle. Pick up 13 st around leg opening. Join and knit every rnd for 45 rnds. Cut yarn, leaving a 10 inch tail, loosely thread through stitches, lightly block leg. Stuff leg, stuffing joint loosely for flexibility, and cinch opening, weaving in ends when finished.

Repeat for the other leg.

Make tail:

Using CC and dpn, pick up 3 st from the center of mouse tushie and work I-cord for 8 inches, cut yarn, draw through st, and weave in ends.

Make outer ear as follows:

Using MC and size 5 needles, CO 9, leaving a 12 inch tail.

Knit 1 row. P3, [pfb] 3 times, p3. Work 4 rows st st.

k2, ssk, k4, k2 tog, k2. Purl next row.

K2, ssk, k2, k2tog, k2. Purl 1 row.

Cut yarn, leaving a 6 inch tail, draw short tail through working stitches, and weave in. Leave longer tail intact. Make 2.

Make inner ear as follows:

Using CC and size 5 needles, CO 7, leaving a 12 inch tail.

K2, [kfb] 3 times, k2. Purl 1 row. Work 4 rows st st.

K2, ssk, k2, k2tog, k2. P3, p2tog, p3.

Cut yarn, leaving a 6 inch tail, draw short tail through working stitches, and weave in. Make 2.

Place lining on ear, purl sides together, and whipstitch lining to outer ear using the CC yarn tail, cupping the ear slightly as shown in photo. Repeat for other ear. Stitch to mouse head using the MC yarn tail, as shown in the photo. Weave in ends.

Finish doll by stitching on eyes and nose. Each eye and the nose are a simple oval shape. Add eyelashes as desired.

Dauphine

This sweet dress for Phoebe Mouse is seamless and is knit in the round from the top down. There is a simple eyelet border at the hemline; feel free to substitute a lace pattern of your choice.

Using the size 5 dpns and CC, CO 45 st. Pm and join for working in the round.

Knit 1 round. Purl 1 round. Knit 3 rounds.

Next row: *k1, yo, k2tog, yo* repeat from * to * across row. 60 st.

Knit 3 rounds. Purl 1 round. Knit 1 round.

Create armhole: p8, BO14pw, p16, BO14pw, p8.

Next row: k8, CO10, k16, CO10, k8. 52 st.

Mark beginning of round, switch to size 7 needles and knit 2 rounds.

Next round: k13, pm, k26, pm, k13.

Increase row: knit to 1 stitch before the 1st marker, m1, k1, slip marker, k1, m1, knit to 1 st before 2nd marker, m1, k1, slip marker, k1, m1, knit to end of row. 56 st.

Knit 4 rounds.

Repeat these last five rounds 6 times more. 80 st.

Purl 1 round. K 2 rounds.

Next row: *k2tog, yo* repeat from * to * across row.

Knit 2 rounds. Purl 1 round.

BO all stitches. Weave in ends. Block lightly.

Phoebe Doll Sweater

Yarn

Brown Sheep Company Lamb's Pride Superwash Bulky [100% wool; 110 y/101m per 100g skein]; color: Mint Cream; approx. 150 yards (1.25 skeins)

Needles

1 set US 10 ½ double-pointed needles or size to obtain correct gauge

24 inch US 10 ½ circular needles

Notions

Stitch holders and removable stitch markers

3 1- inch buttons or frog closures

Gauge

14 sts/16 rows = 4" in stockinette stitch

Pattern Notes

The Phoebe Doll Sweater is knit with the same construction techniques as the girl's version. It is designed to fit Phoebe Mouse, but can easily be modified to fit most 16 to 18-inch dolls by lengthening the hood by an inch or so to allow for a little more ease over the doll's head. You could also substitute frog closures or ties for the buttons if you wish to.

Pattern

Using circular needle, cast on 68 st. Work pattern as follows:

Row 1: p2, *wyib, sl 1 as if to knit, bring yarn to front and p2*; repeat from * to *

Row 2: k2, *wyif, sl 1 as if to purl, bring yarn to back and k2*; repeat from * to *

Row 3: knit

Row 4: purl

Work these four rows twice more.

Work in st st until garment measures 5 inches from the CO edge, ending with a rs row.

Shape Bodice: [p2tog] 6 times, [p2tog, p1] 14 times, [p2tog] 7 times. 41 st rem.

Work rows 1 and 2 of pattern.

Buttonhole row: k2, yo, k2tog, knit rest of row.

Next row: purl.

Work rows 1, 2, and 3 of pattern once more.

Front

Divide for sleeve opening: p10, place on holder, p21, place on holder, p10.

Working on these 10 st for the right front, work rows 1 and 2 of pattern. Repeat buttonhole row. Purl 1 row. Work rows 1-4 of pattern. Work rows 1 and 2 of pattern. Repeat buttonhole row. Purl 1 row. Work rows 1 and 2 of pattern.

Shape neck: BO 5 st, place removable marker, knit rest of row. Purl 1 row. Place all 5 st on holder for shoulder.

Make left front in the same manner, keeping in pattern, reversing shaping, and omitting buttonholes.

Back

Work back and forth on 21 st, keeping in pattern as established, until 1 row shorter than the front. Work 5 st, place on dpn, BO 11 st, work 5 st, place on dpn. Finish shoulder seam on each side using 3-needle bind-off.

Sleeves

Using dpns, pick up 21 st around armhole opening. Knit 10 rnds. Decrease row: * k5, k2tog* three times.

Begin pattern:

Row 1: *wyib, sl 1 as if to knit, bring yarn to front and p2* repeat from * to *

Row 2: *wyib, sl 1 as if to purl, bring yarn to front and p2* repeat from * to *

Rows 3 & 4: knit

Repeat 4 rows of pattern once more. Work row 1 of pattern. BO all st in pattern. Repeat for other sleeve.

Hood

Between removable markers, pick up 22 st. I like to use a crochet hook for this task. With the rs facing you, begin hood at right front edge.

Set-up row: sl1 wyib as if to k, p2, sl1 wyib as if to k, k6, pm, k2, pm, k6, sl1 wyib as if to k, p2, sl1 wyib as if to k.

Next row: sl1 wyif as if to p, k2, sl1 wyif as if to p, purl to last 4 st, sl1 wyif as if to p, k2, sl1 wyif as if to p.

Row 1: Knit to marker, m1, slip marker, k2, slip marker, m1, knit to end of row.

Row 2: Purl

Row 3: sl1 kw, p2, sl1 kw, knit to marker, m1, slip marker, k2, slip marker, m1, knit to last 4 st and sl1 kw, p2, sl1 kw.

Row 4: sl1 pw, k2, sl1 pw, purl to last 4 st, sl1 pw, k2, sl1 pw.

Repeat these four rows once more. 30 st.

Keeping the pattern on the hood edge as worked in these four rows, work straight without shaping for 12 more rows or to desired length.

Place half of hood st on another needle and graft top of hood using kitchener st.

Finishing

Weave in ends. Block. Sew on buttons, frog closures, or ties as you prefer.

abbreviations

beg	beginning
BO	bind off
CO	cast on
dpn	double-pointed needle
k2tog	knit two together
k	knit
kfb	knit in front and back of stitch
kw	knitwise
m1	make one by knitting into the back of the loop just below the next stitch
p2tog	purl two together
p	purl
patt	pattern
pm	place marker
pfb	purl in front and back of stitch
pw	purlwise
rem	remain
rs	right side
sl	slip
st	stitch
sts	stitches
st st	stockinette stitch
ws	wrong side
wyib	with yarn in back
wyif	with yarn in front

Joanna Johnson has a B.A. in Literature from Drew University. She has enjoyed combining her love of books and knitting in this special knitting picture book. She lives in Loveland, Colorado, with her husband and their three children, who are a constant source of inspiration for her stories. This is her first book.

Eric Johnson has a B.F.A. from Kutztown University in Graphic Design. After working in commercial design for two decades as a signwriter, muralist, and graphic designer, he has enjoyed returning to his childhood love of drawing by setting pencil to paper to illustrate this book. He lives with his wife and their three children in Loveland, Colorado. This is his first book.

Yarn Supplier:
Brown Sheep Co, Inc
100662 CR 16
Mitchell, NE 69357
phone 1.800.826.9136
fax 1.308.635.2143
www.brownsheep.com

Acknowledgments
Deepest thanks to: Our family and friends, especially our parents, for listening, loving, and being supportive. The Tuesday Night Knitters, for their friendship and good fun, especially Karen DeGeal, for encouraging me to knit outside my comfort zone. Peggy Jo Wells and Kathy Muhr at Brown Sheep for being so helpful. Natalia Morales, for technical and moral support. Christa Tippmann, my photographer, for capturing time so beautifully. Laurel Anne Johnson and Shiloh Elizabeth Alexandra Bruce, our models, for being so sweet. Hadley Austin, for tech editing the patterns. Katie Himmelberg for editorial guidance. Liz Gipson, for a very helpful conversation. My test knitters, for valuable advice: Jill Motley, for her inquisitiveness; Krista Elston, for her thoughtfulness; Mari January, for her exuberance; Megan Helzer, for her sweetness; Molly Henthorne, for her willingness, and Tedi Cox, for her spontaneity. Last but not least, I am thankful to my husband, children, and God, for inspiring me in the first place.